This book belongs to:

_____

NICK'S SANTA SLEIGH

Cynthia Noles

Illustrated by
John E. Hume, Jr.

Janneck Books
Crescent City, Florida

Book and cover design by Sagaponack Books & Design

CIP Data

ISBNs:
978-1-950434-19-0 (softcover)
978-1-950434-20-6 (hardcover)
978-1-950434-21-3 (e-book)

Library of Congress Control Number: 2019916609

Summary: A young boy who wants to be a Santa's helper asks his dad
to help him build a sleigh so he can deliver toys to children in the town.

JUV017010 Juvenile Fiction / Holidays & Celebrations / Christmas
JUV057000 Juvenile Fiction / Stories in Verse
JUV039220 Juvenile Fiction / Social Themes / Values & Virtues
JUV013030 Juvenile Fiction / Family / Multigenerational

Janneck Books
Crescent City, Florida

Printed and bound in the United States of America
First Edition

Thanks to the following people who have been instrumental in helping me bring this book to light: John and Anne Hume, Peggy Trice, Charles Lane, Beth Mansbridge, and Frances Keiser.

—Cynthia Noles

Thanks to Emma Broullard for allowing her dog Charlie to be my model for Noel in this book.

—John E. Hume, Jr.

To my wonderful family and friends who have encouraged me, and especially Alex, who inspired me to write this story.

—Cynthia Noles

To Kim, Loren, Wayne, Marlene, Nieli, and my sweet wife Anne.

—John E. Hume, Jr.

Nicholas Anderson was a nice young boy

Who always had a dream in his heart:

He wished to be one of Santa's helpers,

And now he felt ready to start!

Nick's father Joseph was a fine engineer.
He enjoyed building things of all kinds:
Skyscrapers, bridges, and hospitals he built
Were structures that boggle our minds.

One day, Nick got the courage to speak

To his dad about building a real Santa sleigh;

It had to be just the right color and size

To contain lots of toys for Christmas Day!

Across the street lived Nick's grandmother.

She watched Nick's project with a smile;

She knew her grandson had lots of imagination,

And this plan seemed pretty wild!

Now, his grandmother was a fine seamstress;

She designed Nick's Santa's helper suit.

Next day, he rushed over to try it on.

Looking in the mirror, he knew he was cute!

Mr. Anderson worked days and some nights

To make his son's dream come true.

The sleigh would be pulled by his tractor

And painted red with a splash of blue.

Word of this young Santa spread all around.
One lady put signs on every corner and street,
Asking for donations for kids in their town.
Boy Santa worked through the cold and the heat!

Neighbors donated toys for many weeks:
There were dolls, computers, books, and bikes,
Skateboards, puzzles, and new board games,
Along with rubber toys for the tykes.

Christmas Eve had finally arrived.

Nick dressed in his perfect red suit.

Then he climbed into his beautiful sleigh—

Suddenly he realized he had only one boot!

Everyone was frantic looking for the boot;

It could not have walked away!

Then grandmother saw it and yelled,

"My dog Noel just hid it in the hay!"

The boy Santa and his helpful dad
Gave away gifts all through the night;
This young man was living his dream
Into the early, bright morning light.

Now, finally, young Nicholas has realized

How it makes people feel, in giving;

No wonder Santa Claus is always jolly,

And certainly, it makes life worth living!

How Well Do You Remember the Story?

1. What is the boy's name?

2. What is the father's name?

3. What is Nick's father's job?

4. What does Joseph build for his job?

5. Does Nick live near his grandmother?

6. What does Nick's grandmother make for him?

7. What color is the sleigh?

8. What pulls the sleigh?

9. What is in the sleigh's sack?

10. What is on the tractor's hood?

11. What does the boy do with the donated toys?

12. How does the sleigh move?

13. What are some of the toys and gifts that are collected?

14. Is there a teddy bear in any of the illustrations?

15. How many teddy bears can you find?

Discussion Questions

1. How do you feel when you receive a gift?

2. How does it make you feel when you give someone else a gift?

3. On what occasions might you give someone a gift?

4. What things might you give as a gift?

5. What is the best gift you ever received and why?

6. What items might *you* build or sew?

7. What might you dream or imagine that you could do to bring joy to others?

8. Are you a helper? Who do you help and what do you do?

9. Do you have a favorite toy?

10. What are some things you can donate?

ABOUT THE AUTHOR

Cynthia Noles has been writing stories and rhymes since she was in the first grade and has continued writing rhyming stories her whole life. She does it for the fun and love of writing and for the pleasure it gives others.

When her neighbor, author and illustrator John Hume read some of her stories, he knew she had to bring them to a wider audience.

Cynthia has two grown sons, lives in Florida, and continues to write two stories each week.

Learn more about Cynthia and her books at JanneckBooks.com.

ABOUT THE ILLUSTRATOR

John E. Hume, Jr. has been drawing since childhood—always with a sense of humor and whimsy.

After receiving a BS from Buffalo State Teachers College, teaching, as well as art, became his passion. He has taught art to students from elementary grades through college, including Flagler College, in St. Johns County, Florida.

John lives in Florida with his wife Anne, where he enjoys writing and illustrating stories about their nine cats, and where he can still balance a yardstick on his nose!

Learn more about John and his books at JanneckBooks.com.